Special Ed

Written by
Barry Rudner

Illustrated by
Peggy
Trabalka

Windword Press

ISBN 0-9642206-6-0

Printed and published in the United States by
Windword Press.
Publisher is in Farmington Hills, MI 48334.
1-800-718-5888
http://www.windwordpress.com

Library of Congress Catalog Card Number: 98-90743

Dedicated to Keith...

Who taught me how
lucky *I* am.

Every once upon a while
nature tips the scale
to give us those
with special needs
and different types of frail.

Their minds remain a child,

or their bodies might be weak.

Their senses are not perfect,

or their learning might be meek.

Much like pegs
that are not round,
they are square, instead.
So often we refer to them
as simply Special Ed.

Special Ed is special
not by fortune
or by fame.
He wears
a lot of faces
and he has
as many names.

We say that he is special
but we treat him like he's not.
As if the meaning
of the word
we simply just forgot.

We say he has a screw loose.
He cannot find just where,
or what the missing part is
when we say he's not all there.

We tease him that he's not too bright.
He never knew he glowed.
We say that he is one brick short
of having a full load.

We also say he's not too swift,
though he runs quite fast.

And even when he's first in line
we seem to pick him last.

We say he's in left field
but he always plays first base,

or has a foggy attic,
yet his house has no such space.

10

What truly makes him special
is he has a quiet will,

to just be seen on equal ground
although he climbs uphill.

11

For Special Ed is special,
he might need an extra hand,

a little time,

a bit more help,

for us to understand,

that everyday's a contest
in a match he knows alone,

to reach,

to think,

or even stand,

to travel on his own.

13

He sometimes rides a chariot
wherever he might go.

He follows by an open hand
to lead him so he knows.

14

He often ties himself in knots
before he does his laces.

On his legs and not his teeth
are where we find his braces.

He wonders if the old man
in the moon ever shaves,

or why the people on TV
do not return his waves.

16

His greatest handicap, it seems,
is how we treat him being,
the way he is,
and how he feels,
to see what he is seeing.

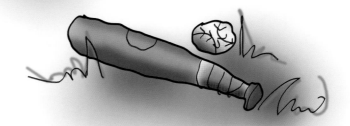

For even though he cannot hear

he still can see words spoken.

He also wishes to be held,

although his touch is broken.

And even though he cannot step

he wishes to advance.

He also still has vision

though he has no sight to glance.

And even with his wrinkled thoughts

they somehow still unfold.

And even with his muscles weak

he has a heart of gold.

His song is not of pity,

nor for us to take his place,

nor thought of as disabled
from the dash called human race.

For everytime we see him
he reminds us how we are,
that fortune is our only crutch
and that he is by far,

well beyond not able
for he lives without a doubt,
what we take for granted
and we do not live without.

So if we soon forget his gift,
remember what we said,
because he still embraces life,
that's why he's Special Ed.